Gold Rush Fever!

Penn Mullin

High Noon Books
Novato, California

Cover Design and Interior Illustrations: Michael Cincotta

International Standard Book Number: 1-57128-116-9

10 09 08 07 06 05 04
2 1 0 9 8 7

A number of High Noon Books, like this *Trailblazers Series*, are particularly appropriate as ancillary social studies materials. This may explain why the *Postcards Series* and the *Four Corners Series* are so very popular. Write for our free High Noon Books catalog that describes these and many other titles.

Contents

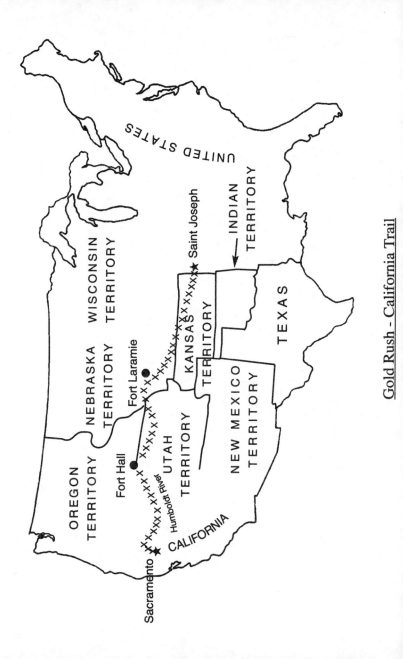

Gold Rush - California Trail

CHAPTER 1

Fort Hall Ahead!

A gold nugget as big as an orange! That's how this all began, Jack thought. One night back home in St. Joe we heard that gold was found in California. Guess I got gold fever right then in '48. Now here I am one year later. I'm 2,000 miles from home. I'm dirty, hot, and tired. Hope it's true about that gold!

Jack sat in the driver's seat of the big wagon. Six oxen were yoked up to pull it.

Oh, no! Looks like that lead ox has a sore

leg, thought Jack. What next? Will she make it to Fort Hall? It's just a mile or so now. From inside the wagon he heard a cry. Meg Long's new baby was awake. She was just two weeks old. Born right before her pa drowned crossing the river. Good thing Carl and I are here to help Meg, Jack thought. Meg's husband had hired them back in St. Joseph, Missouri, last May. That was three months ago.

Just then Carl rode up. "Hope there's mail for us at the fort!" he said.

"You said that at Fort Laramie," Jack laughed. "I think the girls in St. Joe forgot us. Three months is a long time!"

"They better not forget us! I aim to go back

with pockets full of gold!" said Carl.

"I hope there's some left. Fifty thousand folks on the trail this year!" Jack said. "All off to the gold fields!"

"I'll be glad to dig for gold and get rid of these cows! They need to be milked right away." Carl looked back at the small herd.

"How many wagons in our train will go with us to California?" Jack asked.

"Twenty, I think. Some of those bound for Oregon have changed their minds. Must be gold fever," said Carl.

"Look! Smoke ahead. Campfires. Can't be far to Fort Hall," Jack said.

Just then Meg came out of the wagon and

sat beside Jack. She held her tiny baby, Claire, on her lap. Jack saw that Meg had put on a new sunbonnet and a clean dress. Her face was tanned dark and covered with insect bites.

"It will be good to see some new folks here," Meg said. "Maybe there will be mail from home, too." She smiled.

"Yes, ma'am," said Carl. "That's what we hope. And I want to get some hard candy. And a new shirt."

"We're low on coffee and sugar," Meg said. "It's been a long time since I baked you boys a pie."

Jack smiled. It was good to see Meg feel better. Her husband's death had been an awful shock for her.

Now they could see the square log fort ahead on the flat plains. Many Paiute (PIE-ute) tepees stood around it and perhaps a hundred wagons. Their white canvas tops snapped in the wind.

"Are they all going to the gold fields?' asked Meg.

"Most of them, ma'am. This is the last place to stock up for the trail south," Jack told her.

Soon the Paiutes came up with buffalo robes and pieces of fresh salmon.

Carl said, "That salmon looks real good! Those robes will be nice and warm this winter.

Do you want one, ma'am?"

"Yes. Let's give them flour and beans for it," Meg said. "They look hungry."

Soon baby Claire was wrapped up in the thick buffalo robe. The Paiutes all smiled and came up close to see her.

Jack stopped the wagon and unyoked the oxen to graze. Then he and Carl began to milk the cows. "We'll see you up at the fort!" they called to Meg. She put Claire in a basket. Then the two of them set off for the big open gates of Fort Hall.

CHAPTER 2

A Choice for Meg

People crowded in and out of the fort. Meg saw Indians, cavalry soldiers, emigrants from the wagon trains. Oxen bawled, dogs barked, men yelled. Trappers carried huge loads of beaver pelts. Meg looked at the long line at the post office. She would come back later. There was a line for food, too. Men scooped coffee, sugar, beans, rice, and flour out of big barrels. Meg bought the things on her list. Then she saw a table full of fresh squash and potatoes. She

*Then she saw a table full of fresh squash
and potatoes.*

8

could almost taste them. She filled her sack. Then she saw the price.

"Who would pay that much for a potato?" she asked the man.

"You will if you want one," he laughed. "That's the last potato you'll see till you get to the gold fields."

Meg frowned and took out her purse. She had little choice. They still had nearly two months left to go. And she knew Jack and Carl were tired of beans and bacon.

Soon she was in the mail line again. "A letter for Mrs. Charles Long?"

Meg's heart jumped. A letter from home from her parents. She took it to a quiet bench.

"*Dearest Meg and Charles*," it began. Meg felt hot tears rush to her eyes. Of course, they didn't know about Charles. How could they? She read on. If only she could see her parents! She should go back. There was no reason to go to the gold fields now. Charles was gone. Maybe someone at the fort was turning back. She and Claire could go with them. Jack and Carl could have the wagon and go on. Yes, that was the best plan. Now she just had to find someone going east.

Crowds went by. Voices reached her. "Forty-Mile Desert . . . Lost ten oxen . . . Some folks went crazy from thirst . . . Crossed the Sierras . . . We almost turned back. But so glad we didn't . . . Staked a claim in California. Found gold . . . Built a cabin . . ."

Meg thought about a claim, a cabin, California. She remembered what Charles had wanted for her and Claire. What he had worked so hard for. Lost his life for. How could she just give up what he had dreamed of? No, she would not turn back. She would make it on her own in California. Later on she might go back east. But first she would follow Charles's plan.

Meg picked up Claire and set off for her wagon. She had a pie to bake tonight!

CHAPTER 3

"Tie Things Down!"

"There's the Humboldt!" Jack pointed to the river ahead. It wound its way out into the wide flat valley. "Looks like there's lots of good grass all along it, too."

"We follow it for 350 miles," Carl said. "Till it ends in a swamp. Then we start out on the Forty-Mile Desert!"

"Then we cross the Sierra Mountains," Meg joined in. "I can't wait to put my feet on California soil!"

"Hope there's still room for us to stake a claim there," said Carl. "Look how many folks joined us at Fort Hall!" He pointed to the long line of wagons ahead.

Just then they heard the call "Nooner!" It was passed all along the wagons. Time to eat and rest. Jack and Carl stopped the wagon by the river. They let loose the cows and oxen to drink. Meg looked for wood to start a fire. Then she sliced up some of the potatoes to fry. She'd saved them for a surprise.

"That smells so fine, ma'am! Are those *potatoes*?" Jack stared into the black fry pan that stood on three legs.

"Potatoes! This helps make up for no mail

at the fort," Carl said. He picked up baby Claire and rocked her. She cried softly.

"I don't like the looks of those clouds," Jack said. "We're in for a storm."

"Hope it holds off till we have these potatoes!" Carl said.

They sat down in the shade of the wagon to eat.

"This sure is a feast, ma'am," Carl told Meg. He reached for a biscuit. "I never thought I'd have these on the trail."

"The trail captain wants to make 23 miles a day on this part of the trail," Jack said. "Then we'll reach the desert in about two weeks. That will be mid-August. I know he's scared of snow in the mountains. We all know about that poor Donner group that got trapped."

Meg felt a chill go down her back. She knew the dreadful tale well. The Donner group was stuck for the whole winter in the snow. Many of them had died. Folks talked of this all the time on the trail. No one wanted that awful fate. The best thing was to just keep *moving*. That's what the trail captain told them each day.

"I can feel fall is closer," Carl said. "There's a chill in the morning."

Meg pulled her shawl close around her. The wind began to tear at the canvas wagon top.

"It's gettin' set to blow," said Jack. "We better tie things down. Get the stock all in and

15

tied up, too. Don't want them to spook and run off."

Meg put all the food and dishes away. This all fit snug in a box on the back of the wagon. Next she put baby Claire's basket inside. A light rain began to fall.

The trail captain rode up and said to put the wagons in a big circle. The stock would go in the middle. Jack yolked up the oxen and moved the wagon. Then Carl pounded wood stakes into the ground. He tied the wagon to them with ropes. "This sure won't blow over now!" he said.

The stock were bawling in fear. They could sense that a storm was near.

Then the rain began to pound down. Meg jumped into the wagon. Carl and Jack went under it. Baby Claire started to scream. Meg rocked her as the wind roared. She could hear the rain tear at the canvas top above. She had never heard rain so hard. Would the wagon top hold? Her heart hammered with fear.

Just then Jack jumped inside. "Come under the wagon. It's a hailstorm. It will come through the top." He reached out for Claire. Now there was a pounding sound above. Hail the size of walnuts! "Come on!" Jack cried. He wrapped Claire in the buffalo robe. They jumped out the back of the wagon and rolled under it. Meg felt her face sting as the hail hit her.

They lay under the wagon. The hailstones slammed down. Soon the ground was white. They could see the cattle standing with their heads down and eyes shut. The hail beat down on them.

When will it stop? thought Meg. Has it soaked through the top of the wagon? Will all our things be ruined? Why did I think I could do this? I should have turned back at the fort.

Lightning flashed. The stock went wild. Horses, cows, and oxen raced around in the center of the wagons. They found an open space. Then they raced out of the circle onto the plains into the storm.

CHAPTER 4

Visitors

Meg dragged the heavy soaked quilts out of the wagon. She spread them on the grass to dry. If only the sun would stay out awhile. Everyone needed to dry things. The hail had torn the canvas tops. Clothes and bedding were soaked. The trail captain gave them only one day to rest and dry out. They had to find their lost stock, too.

Jack and Carl had gone off to find the lost cows and oxen. Who knew how far the stock had run in the storm? What if they could not be found? There were only three oxen left now to pull the wagon. Could they do it? Meg stared out over the flat plains all around her. But she could see no riders.

Just then she heard a noise behind her! She turned to see two Shoshone (Sho-SHOW-nee) women there. Each had a papoose strapped to her back. They smiled and then pointed to their mouths. They're hungry, Meg said to herself. And they're so thin! She made signs with her hands for them to come with her. From her wagon she gave them flour, sugar, bacon, and beans. They smiled and gave Meg some bright blue beads. Meg thanked them and admired how quiet their babies were. Just their tiny faces

Meg turned to see two Shoshone women. Each had a papoose strapped to her back.

showed. They were wrapped up tight to their chins in cloth. Then they were strapped to a cradleboard worn on the back. When Meg showed them Clair, they touched her golden hair. Then they left, holding their new food tight. They joined other Shoshones who had come to the wagons.

Meg watched them go and felt sad. Her own life was hard, but at least she would always have enough to eat. Claire would, too. But then a sudden thought hit Meg. Her money from Charles would run out in a few months. What then? What if she never found any gold? How would she earn money? Well, she could sew. She could cook. She would hire herself out to work. She would make it. She just had to.

"So the Shoshones came to call on you, too?" said a voice. It was Rose, from the next wagon.

Meg said, "Yes, they were very friendly. "

"Most Indians we've seen on this trip just want food. Some even helped us cross the river!" said Rose.

Just then they heard a shout. The men were coming back with the stock! Soon Jack and Carl rode up. "We found three oxen! Not so lucky with the cows. Only brought three back."

Meg felt her heart jump. She had counted on the cows for California. She knew she could sell them for a lot of money there. But at least the oxen were safe. Without them the wagon could not cross the mountains.

The quilts and bedding dried in the warm sun. Meg mended the torn wagon top while Claire slept. Rose came over to sew quilt squares after lunch. She and Meg had each brought pieces of cloth from home. Later these would all be sewn into quilts.

At the end of the day someone brought out a fiddle. The sound of soft voices and music filled the air. Meg sang along with the tune she knew well by now:

There's plenty of gold

So I've been told,

On the banks of the Sacramento!

24

CHAPTER 5

The "Sink"

"What's that awful smell?" Meg looked out over the prairie. She rode beside Jack on the wagon seat. "Is it bad water?"

"Right. It's the Sink," Jack said. "The Humboldt has ended in a swamp."

"Is that long, hot desert ahead of us now?" Meg looked out to the west. All she could see was an endless flat plain.

"Yes. The captain will give us a rest on the first day," said Jack. "But there won't be much rest. We have to cut a lot of grass to take for the stock. Then load up water. There's no water or grass for forty miles."

The wagon train soon made camp. The captain warned that the water in the Sink was poison. They must not drink it or let the stock near it. Water should come from nearby springs ahead. Meg filled each pot and bucket she had with water. People cut armloads of tall grass. They filled their wagons with it.

Meg baked bread and beans for the trip. There would be no time to stop and cook on the desert. Mosquitoes swarmed around her as she worked. Claire cried most of the day. They were all too busy to sit and rock her. The wagons must be all set to leave at dusk. That way they could make many miles by sunrise.

There was a meeting before they left. "I want to cross this desert in two days," the captain said. "Your water will go fast. The oxen have to drink so much to keep going. Our rest stops will be short. Don't get spread out. And watch for the hot springs at night. They boil up out of the ground. You can walk right into them."

How awful, thought Meg. She would ride at night as much as she could. She helped Carl load in the last bunch of grass. Then she picked up Claire and climbed up on the wagon seat next to Jack. Carl rode behind with the cows.

They set off into the desert as the sun went down. The air was cool now, and the mosquitoes were gone at last. Meg held a cold cloth to the bites on Claire's arms. "I sure hope we have enough water," Jack said.

"We filled every pot we had," Meg said. "That's all we can do." She gazed out over the endless flat sands. Here and there was a lone cactus. Her eyes searched far ahead for the high Sierras. She knew they were out there, waiting. The last hurdle to cross.

CHAPTER 6

The Forty-Mile Desert

Dawn broke. With it came the heat. The sun blazed down. There was a short stop to water the stock and eat breakfast. The sand was hard and crusty. People's faces were coated with dust.

"Take a good long drink, ma'am," Carl told Meg. "This sun can just dry you up." He held out the water dipper to her.

Meg's throat was so dry it hurt to swallow. But she knew she must drink.

29

The oxen sucked long and hard at the water in the buckets. Carl knew it would not last if they drank like this each time. They still had a long way to go.

On and on the wagons rolled in the hot sun. The oxen strained and moaned.

The captain called for a rest at supper time. Jack and Carl unyoked the oxen. Meg set out cold beans and bread.

Just then Meg heard the sound of cattle running. Jack yelled, "The stock broke loose! They smelled water in the spring. But it's poison!" He and Carl raced off on their horses. Meg tied up the two oxen that were left. Her heart pounded with fear. What would they do if all their stock died?

Jack and Carl soon were back. Their faces were grim. They led the cows and oxen behind them.

"The stock were deep in it," Carl told Meg. "Don't know how much they drank. All we can do is hope. The next few hours will tell if they live or die."

The captain said they should not make the stock move now. The wagons would wait a few hours. There was a mood of gloom over the camp. People knew they might not get over the mountains.

Meg tried to keep busy. She made a fire out of dry sage she had found. Then she put coffee on to boil and made biscuits.

Carl and Jack sat and stared at the stock. Which ones would fall over first?

A few hours passed and dusk came on. Then the lead ox went down on her knees. Jack rushed to her side. Her eyes looked crazed. She moaned with pain. Then one of the cows went down. A short time later two more oxen dropped. The same thing went on at many wagons.

The captain rode up. "How many did you lose?" he asked Meg.

"Four," she told him.

"You might still make it with three," he said. "But if you lose one more . . ."

CHAPTER 7

Up the Truckee

"Look, Meg! The end of the desert! There's the river! Look at those mountains!" Jack pointed ahead. "California!" He let out a whoop of joy.

"At last!" Meg stared ahead. She could see thick green grass and trees. Hills and then high snowy peaks beyond. How could they ever get the wagons over them? But on the far side was their new home. They would find a way!

Oxen were unyoked and ran to the river. The people ran, too. The cold clear water felt so good. Meg dunked her whole head in. "We're almost there!" she said. "Just the mountains. Then we'll be in the *gold* country! I just wish Charles were here with us now."

"He'd be glad you're still on the trail," said Jack. "You'll set up your place in California. Just like he wanted."

Soon they were back on the trail. It followed the winding Truckee River. The river had been named for the Paiute chief who first guided people this way.

It was slow going. In one mile they had to cross the river ten times! People wanted to rest. But the captain pushed on. He feared what an early snow could do.

Now they climbed through narrow canyons. The trail was steep and rocky.

"We may have to lighten our load," Jack said. "Or the stock won't hold out."

"We'll do it at the lake where the Donners were," Carl said. "It's close."

Meg felt a chill when she heard the word "Donner." It was just three years ago that so many people had died at this lake.

Soon they were there. Meg gasped when she saw the huge snowy peaks of the Sierras. They rose up like a wall at the end of the lake. She could not see how a wagon could cross this wall. Or a person! She saw no sign of a trail.

"There's what's left of the Donner cabins,"

Meg started to help unload.

Jack pointed to piles of logs near the shore of the lake. "Starvation Camp."

Meg shivered. She wanted to leave this gloomy place. But the captain said they should lighten their wagons here. They would start up the mountains at dawn. Meg knew what "lighten" meant. She must leave things behind. And the things she loved most were heavy. Claire's cradle. Ma's oak rocker. The trunk full of dishes. Meg started to help unload.

They watched the sun set behind the Sierras. Soon the sky was filled with a pink glow. Meg knew that California was behind those mountains. She was so near. Yet still so far.

CHAPTER 8

Over the Top

They left at dawn. Meg turned one last time to look at the things she had left behind. Then she turned her face towards the mountains. The captain knew the way they should cross. He had done it before.

"Double-team the oxen up the steep parts," he said. "Lend oxen back and forth between you. Only the drivers ride. Carry what you can. Make the load lighter."

Meg walked behind the wagon and carried

Claire. Jack drove while Carl pulled the horse and the cows. Each carried things tied to its back.

The trail was steep now. The lake looked very small below them.

Suddenly the wagons stopped. "There's a wall of rock ahead," Jack yelled. "Can't get the wagons through."

Word came down to unyoke the oxen. There was a hole in the rock big enough for them. But not for a wagon. Men took the stock through the hole one by one. Then people went through.

How will we ever get the wagons up? thought Meg. The rock wall was so high.

The oxen were up on top of the wall now. Men hitched them to the wagons below with chains. First they took off the wagon tops. Then the oxen pulled the wagons up. Men helped push from down below. It was scary to watch. The men would be crushed if a wagon fell.

Soon all the wagons were up. They were on the trail again. It was steeper now. Jack and Carl borrowed two oxen from a wagon that had eight.

There were more rock walls to climb. Wagons had to be unloaded and loaded again and again. Tempers flared. People were tired. They wanted to reach the top by nightfall. One could not camp on this narrow trail.

Meg's legs ached. She had blisters on both heels. Carl helped carry Claire. I sure will miss the boys when they leave, Meg thought. What a help they've been! It was hard to believe. The long trip was nearly over. She would be in California tonight! But right now all she could do was put one foot before the other.

Hours passed. A cold wind blew down from the mountain tops. It could snow up here any time now. The captain knew this well.

Meg picked her way through the rocks on the trail. Step after step.

Suddenly she heard a cheer. It rang down the trail from wagon to wagon. They had reached the top! Just a few more steps and she tumbled into a wide green meadow. She lay down with Claire in the deep grass.

Jack and Carl ran up. "We did it!" they yelled and threw their hats in the air. "Gold fields, here we come!" Meg took off her bonnet and threw it into the air, too. She was in California at last!

The wagons all camped in the meadow that night. They would start down the mountains the next day. All the talk was of gold. Groups would split off soon. Some for Bear Valley. Some for Grizzly Flats. Some for Sutter's Mill on the American River. That's where the first nugget of gold had been found last year.

Meg's head was full of names. Gold

diggings like Angel's Camp, Last Chance, Fiddletown. Or Sutter's Fort for supplies.

A man came up to their campfire. "You boys want to strike it rich?" he asked Jack and Carl. "Join up with me. I've got a claim on the Yuba River full of gold!"

"Thanks, but we've got our own place in mind," Jack said. Carl nodded.

"Where's that?" Meg asked.

"Wherever *you* end up, ma'am," said Carl. "We figure we'll stick with you for awhile. Been lucky so far. Good chance we three could strike it rich!"

Meg sat up straight. "Do you mean it? You want to start out gold hunting with me?" She

43

couldn't believe her ears.

"If you'll have us," they told her.

"We'll be partners, then!" Meg said, smiling. "Where shall we start out?"

"How about Carson Hill?"

"Rough and Ready?"

Meg laughed. "I think we need to call our first meeting. And I guess we should make Claire a partner, too! The gold country needs us women!"